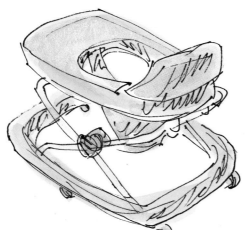

ROLLING ROSE
BY JAMES STEVENSON

 Greenwillow Books, New York

Watercolor paints and a black pen
were used for the full-color art.
The text type is ITC Usherwood.

Printed in Hong Kong by South China
Printing Company (1988) Ltd.
First Edition   10 9 8 7 6 5 4 3 2

Library of Congress Cataloging-in-Publication Data

Stevenson, James (date)
Rolling Rose / by James Stevenson.
      p.   cm.
Summary: When no one is looking, Rose rolls out the door
in her stroller and joins eighty-four other babies
in a parade into the country.
ISBN 0-688-10674-9.
ISBN 0-688-10675-7 (lib. bdg.)
[1. Babies—Fiction.]   I. Title.
PZ7.S84748Ro   1992
[E]—dc20   90-24169   CIP   AC

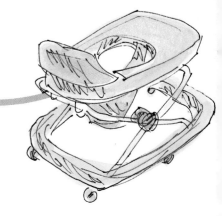

*R*ose rolls around in her Rosemobile.

She rolls to her right.

She rolls to her left.

She rolls to where the cookies are.

She rolls to see Chelsea.

She rolls to see Luke.

She rolls to a stop and she rests.

But one day…
when she rolled to her mother,
her mother was cooking.
When she rolled to her father,
her father was reading.
When she rolled to her brother,
her brother was playing.
When she rolled to see Chelsea,
Chelsea was sleeping.
So Rose rolled and rolled
till she rolled out the door.

She rolled to the garden
and smelled all the flowers.
She rolled to the tree
where Luke liked to swing.
She watched the leaves tremble.
She watched the clouds floating.
She looked at the shadows
slide over the grass.

Rose rolled to the gate,
and the gate was wide open.
She rolled down the sidewalk
and rolled through the people.
They all tried to catch her,
but Rose rolled too fast.

When Matthew saw Rose,
Matthew rolled along with her.
Then Robby came rolling,
and Ruthie came rolling,
and Michael and Debbie
and Donald did, too.

By the time they had traveled
for five or ten minutes,
there were eighty-five babies
in Rose's parade.
When they rolled past the houses,
it sounded like thunder.
Rattling the windows,
they rolled out of town.

They rolled down the highway.
They rolled over bridges.
They bumped and they bounced
down an old country road.

They came to a meadow
and waved to the cows there.
They came to a cornfield
and rolled down the rows.
They rolled to a hilltop
and looked at the view there.

But rain clouds were coming,
and soon rain was falling.
So eighty-five babies
raced home through the rain.
They plowed through the puddles.
They sloshed to their houses.
Up to her front door
Rose slithered and slid.